to Letizia Galli

British Library Cataloguing in Publication Data
Easton, Violet
  Elephants never jump.
  I. Title   II. Solé Vendrell, Carme
  823′.914[J]   PZ7

ISBN 0-86264-109-8

Elephants Never Jump

Story by Violet Easton
Pictures by Carme Solé Vendrell

Andersen Press · London
Hutchinson of Australia

Grocer Badger was adding up Mrs Sheep's bill.

"Three and three are six, and two make BOOO!" and the "Booo!" he shouted at the top of his voice. Poor Mrs Sheep nearly jumped out of her skin. Mrs Goose, who was waiting to be served, jumped almost to the ceiling, and Grocer Badger laughed and laughed.

"That's the third time I've made you jump this week!" he said.

At about that time Mrs Pig was happily hanging out the washing while her husband sat nearby reading a paper. Suddenly Benjamin Leopard leaped out of the bushes. He was wearing a mask and he roared a terrible roar.

Mrs Pig jumped right up into the washing. Mr Pig jumped out of the deckchair and spilt his tea, while Benjamin Leopard laughed even louder than Grocer Badger.

That was the day that the elephant came to live in the village. The animals were saying hello to their new neighbour when the cow shouted, "BOOO!" and made the lion jump while the others all burst out laughing.

"Don't you mean *mooo*?" frowned the elephant.

"It's a game we play," giggled Mrs Pig. "Making each other jump."

"Oh," said the elephant. "Well, elephants never jump."

"Never jump?" gasped the animals together.

"Never," said the elephant. "There are two things that elephants never do: they never jump and they never forget."

That made the animals very excited and as soon as the elephant was out of earshot they agreed to have a competition to see who could make the elephant jump.

The next day the elephant was out walking when, with a roar, the lion sprang from behind a rock. The roar made Sally Goat jump from where she was hiding, also waiting to shout, "Booo!"

"Are you all right?" the elephant asked the lion.

"Yes, thank you," said the lion looking embarrassed. "Actually I was trying to make you jump."

"I told you," said the elephant. "Elephants never jump."

For the next few days it was one thing after another as the animals tried to make the elephant jump.

"Please," said Grocer Badger. "No tricks in the shop. If he jumps in here it will be a disaster."

Then he himself forgot and loudly shouted, "Booo!" at the elephant.

Luckily it didn't work.

The animals no longer tried to make each other jump. It had to be the elephant or nothing, and it wasn't just in the daytime that they tried.

One night, just as the elephant was about to put out the light, two chickens appeared at his window. They squawked and flapped as if they were horrible ghosts.

"Elephants never jump," yawned the elephant, "and even more so at bedtime." Then he put out the light and the chickens felt very silly.

Gradually, as the animals could think of no new tricks to try, the days became peaceful. On one of these peaceful days the elephant and some other animals were having a picnic near the river. Tea was almost ready when a loud "HELP!" came from the water. The tiger twins had found a boat to play in but the mooring rope had come undone. The animals ran to the river to see the boat drifting faster and faster downstream. It was now closer to the other side of the river so that even the long trunk of the elephant could not reach it.

"They're heading for the waterfall!" gasped Grocer Badger. "Quick – back to the bridge. It's the only way to reach them."

"It's too far. We'll never get there in time," cried Mrs Pig as the animals in a panic raced back to the bridge. Only the elephant didn't go with the others.

While the others headed for the bridge the elephant ran away from the river, stopped, turned, and then ran back to the river at full speed. Then, with a fantastic jump, he went high in the air and landed on the other side of the water. Stretching out his trunk he pulled the boat with the twins safely up on to the river bank.

When the other animals arrived they found the twins safe and sound with the elephant.

"How did you get here?" gasped Grocer Badger.

"He jumped, he jumped!" said the twins excitedly. "We've won the competition. We made him jump."

"But," said the lion, "you said elephants never jump."

"I know," said the elephant shyly. "But I forgot."